Lily & THE BOYS

Lily & THE BOYS

JEFF NECESSARY

urlink
PRINT & MEDIA

1603 Capitol Ave., Suite 310 Cheyenne, Wyoming USA 82001
1-888-980-6523 | admin@urlinkpublishing.com

URLink Print and Media is committed to excellence in the publishing industry.

Book design copyright © 2018 by URLink Print and Media. All rights reserved.

Published in the United States of America
ISBN 978-1-64367-056-0 (Paperback)
ISBN 978-1-64367-057-7 (Digital)

Fiction
21.09.18

Never once, while riding buses from ballpark to ballpark many years ago, did Jeff Necessary imagine he'd ever read a children's book, much less write one. Jeff has learned that with time, patience, and a willingness to take a chance, incredible things can happen. Allowing three young puppies into his carefree home was quite a chance, but it completely changed his life . . . for the better. Jeff jokingly says that, "Dogs are so much better than people." His closest friends aren't so sure he's joking about that. They're pretty sure he means it.

Jeff is originally from a very small town in southwestern Virginia. He excelled in sports, especially baseball. From plastic bats and spirited games in the backyard, to being selected by the Pittsburgh Pirates in the amateur baseball draft, to becoming a two time All-American and Hall of Fame member (2014) at King University, in Bristol Tn. Jeff sums up his athletic career by saying only, "I did ok."

These days Jeff teaches Current Events and Civics at North Myrtle Beach High School, plays golf as often as possible, along with caring for his beloved dogs. A 27 year teaching veteran, he still loves being in the classroom. His students know that they will laugh, they will learn, they will hear a wide variety of stories, but most importantly they know that Jeff genuinely cares about them. Jeff has proven that learning can take place along with a whole lot of fun.

Jeff sums it up this way . . . . "I work in a great school surrounded by wonderful people, I have a couple nice sets of golf clubs and access to nearly 100 golf courses, and when I go home I have the sweetest dogs in the world. At least for right now, I'm right where I want to be."

Chapter 1

My Forever Home

Hello, dog lovers! This is your lucky day. You are going to learn all about me and my silly brothers. I think you are going to like me. I'm pretty awesome, or "pawsome", you might say.

My name is Lily. As you can see, I am absolutely adorable. My coat is as white as snow. I'm a Rat Terrier and Yellow Lab mixed together. I like to say I'm "the best of the best." Don't you agree?

I have a wonderful life. But it hasn't always been that way. You might say I got a pretty "ruff" start. That's where my story begins – at the very beginning...

When I was very small, just eight weeks old, I was in an animal shelter. A shelter is an orphanage for animals. I was there because I didn't have a home or a family to love me.

I remember it was really loud at the animal shelter. The big dogs there barked all day and all night. I kept asking, "With all this yapping, how can a girl get any beauty sleep?" They didn't care about my beauty sleep though. They just kept barking. It was very annoying.

I was very small and quiet. I was actually even a little bit shy too. One day a nice man came to the shelter. He was looking at all the dogs, biggest to littlest.

He started out with the big dogs. They were barking really loud, as usual. They wanted to get his attention. And...they did!

Then, the nice man walked to the small dog kennels. That was where I was. I knew I couldn't compete. There was no way I could bark as loud as the big dogs. So I just shyly turned away. But GUESS WHAT?!?!

That nice man became my human! I'm not even kidding. He now describes the moment we met as "love at first sight." He fell in love with me. I fell in love with him right back. My life would never be the same.

My human took me to my new home. It was pawsitively incredible, like heaven on earth. I was the princess of the castle, and I was so happy. I had everything a pup could want. I had toys galore. I had quiet toys, snuggly toys, and loud toys that squeaked too.

And talk about treats! I got a treat every time I went outside to go potty. I got a treat for coming back in too. I got a treat when my human left and even when he came back home. Golly, I got a treat just for being cute. I had it made!

Want to hear about being spoiled? Well, I never cared much for eating out of a bowl, especially a bowl that is on the floor. That's kind of disgusting, don't you think? My human fed me straight from his hands, and he still does. I think that's the way it should be...for a princess pup, at least.

My back yard is absolutely pawsome. I have lots of green grass for my playtime. There is even a fence to keep me safe. It keeps me in and the big, scary dogs out.

My human took me for walks every day. He called it our 'bonding time'. I just called it 'fun time!'

I had my very own bed. My human thought it was his bed too...but really, it was just mine. I am really nice so I shared it with him. Don't you think that was sweet of me?

Each day when my human was at work, or off playing golf somewhere, a really sweet lady who lives across the street came to see if I needed anything. Her name is Mary and she has plenty of experience petting pups. We got along just swell. Sometimes Mary and I shared secrets, but I didn't tell my human. It's a girl thing. Boys just wouldn't understand. I was an "only pup" for a while. It was all about me, and I loved it. I mean...wouldn't you? I had my human's undivided attention, just as a princess should. I lapped it all up. But... that was all about to change.

Chapter 2

Brothers Are Brothers

It's crazy how much a pup can get spoiled in just a few short months. Even when my human went to work, he managed to spoil me. He always left plenty of healthy treats for me and even kept the television on to keep me company. Cartoons were my favorites to watch.

I would hear my human's car drive up in the afternoon and my heart would flutter. The long wait was over. It was time for some spoiling.

One day, I heard him drive up, as usual. My heart was going 'pitter-patter.' I ran to the door to greet him as I always did. This time, however, there was a problem. My human was not alone.

"Oh no!" I thought. "It simply cannot be."

There was a pup in the car with him. And not just any pup...it was one of the annoying pups from the shelter. It was Blazer!

I never liked that big bully. He was obnoxious and stingy too. He never shared any of his treats or toys with the rest of us. "How did he find my human?" I wondered. "Why is he here?" Then I decided the answer was clear. He had come to take everything I had...my toys, my bed...my human. I was mad and sad all at the same time.

My human walked in leading Blazer beside him on a leash.

"Lily, I want you to meet your new brother," he told me.

My fur stood straight up. My...what? How could such an odd looking creature be even remotely related to me, a princess? I was insulted.

Blazer was a mixed up mix of a breed. If I had to guess, I would say he was a little part Basset Hound and a whole bunch of Bully Terrier. Well, maybe that's not a breed. Is Rascal a breed? If so, that is what he is...Rascal and Basset Hound.

There was absolutely no way the super-short creature that stood before me could be my brother. Besides, he was crazy-colored, like he'd been patched together. I figured he probably was.

And I was sure I couldn't trust him. How could I be friends with someone so different from me, let alone be his sister? But my human was dead set on Blazer and me bonding. I was going to need to chew on the idea for a while.

I took my time. The first night was really tough. My human had bought Blazer a bed. He sat it next to the one he had bought for me that I had forgotten all about. I HAD a bed...the big bed. But no, now I was expected to sleep in my dog bed. Really? On the floor?

I tried to warm up to my human's wishes but Blazer was no help at all. He snored all night long. He stopped snoring only when there was a noise outside, like a car driving past. Then he would wake up, bark, then go back to sleep. It was a very, very long night.

While I chewed on the annoying thought of being his sister, or at least his friend, Blazer chewed on everything else. When my human went to work the next day, Blazer proceeded to chew up his favorite pair of golf shoes and two of his prize hats. He ate the remote control, destroyed both ends of the super soft sofa, and even gnawed on a couple rugs too. And that was just the first day!

13

Needless to say, my human wasn't happy when he got home. He was very nice about it though. He put us out in the backyard and said, "I think it would be a good idea for the two of you to get some energy out." For real? *Both* of us?

You will never believe what happened next. As it would turn out, Blazer was a digger. He dug for moles. He dug for bones. He dug just for the sake of digging too. The yard was a gigantic mess in no time flat. But that was not the worst thing.

14

What horrified me, and my human, was when Blazer went digging for moles and caught one. He proudly pranced to the porch with the squirming critter clutched in his teeth. He was sure he had done a great deed but our reactions assured him otherwise.

Blazer is no longer allowed to deliver moles to the porch for which I am thankful. Moles are icky. Don't you agree?

Some things sure had changed. Used to be, when my human went to work, the hours would just creep by as I was all alone. But now they were flying past. Blazer was keeping me very entertained, even if it was with his mischief.

Mary came to visit us a lot. She was the very best, but I had to share her with that rascal, Blazer. Heck, even he behaved when she was around. Mary must have had the magic touch to tame Blazer's wily ways.

One evening, my human brought a swimming pool home. It was just a plastic kiddie one. He thought we might enjoy taking a dip in it to cool off, he said.

Blazer began to bark at the pool. He barked and barked and barked and...barked. That was when it hit me. Blazer wasn't just trying to get on my last nerve with all his barking, he was afraid of the pool. He was trying to bark it away. Maybe he wasn't so scary after all. Was he trying to protect me?

Sometimes, when we were out in the yard, Blazer would run past me playfully. He would stop and crouch down with his back end in the air, wagging his funny furry tail. He wanted to play...with me!

And so we played. We played and we played and we played some more. We played every day. And when we were tired, I shared my comfy bed with him. Sometimes, we slept back to back which was nice, especially when it was cold because he kept me warm.

It really didn't matter anymore that Blazer was different. Sure, he had patchwork colors and I was snow white. He was short and I was... well, not *as* short. He was loud and I was not. We could be buddies.

And so it was that Blazer and I became the best of friends. In fact, we became such close friends, we decided to make a pact. We would be self- proclaimed brother and sister.

We were a team, like peanut-butter and jelly. We were as happy as could be. Little did we know that things were about to turn very, very blue.

Chapter 3
We're So Blue

As I got to know my new brother better and better, things I learned about Blazer's past made me sad. It turned out that our home was his third try at a home. I knew he was worried it wouldn't work out.

The first human that adopted Blazer wasted no time in taking him right back to the shelter. The second one did the same. He was just too much for them.

"Third time's a charm," I tried to tell him in my own furry way.

It seemed like the better life got, the more nervous Blazer grew. Belly-rubs, toys, treats and delicious dinners seemed too good to be true, in his book. He was always suspicious of being taken back to the shelter.

In what seemed like no time at all, he had been at my house for six whole months. That was a record for Blazer. He finally became more secure and realized that he had truly found his forever home.

Blazer wasn't the perfect dog like I was. He got into trouble from time to time and had to be reminded of the rules. Still, he knew he was loved. He learned that being naughty didn't mean he would have to return to the shelter. That was simply not ever going to happen.

I was happy I had learned not to judge a book by its cover or, in my case, a dog by his crazy colored fur. Blazer and I were as different as night and day but boy, oh boy, did we love to play. Tug-o-war was our favorite game.

One day when we were playing tug-o-war, our human drove up. As usual, our tails began to wag and our hearts went pitter-pat. But a closer look turned our rosy world...blue. "Oh no, not another pup!" I said to Blazer. This new pup was as black as I was white. Even though he was just a pup, we knew that he would grow to be as tall as Blazer was short. And his eyes...one was brown and the other one was blue! His coat glistened in the summer sun as our human let him out of the backseat of the car. We were...in big trouble.

Why had our human brought home this handsome puppy? Blazer was sure he was being traded off. He was destined to go back to the shelter. I was wondering if my fate would be the same.

"Come and meet your new brother," our human called to us. Our... what? Surely this dog was not staying. Oh but...he was! Shortly after he arrived, our human decided to name him "Blue" because of his blue eye. That seemed very fitting to us because this new addition to the family certainly made Blazer and me very "blue."

Soon it was dinner time. It was never a problem for Blazer and me. We just ate our food and that was that. But Blue and Blazer instantly went at it. Each was sure the other one was going to try to steal the other's food. Our human quickly put a stop to that nonsense though. There was no need to worry because there was plenty of food, he assured. Even still, our human continued to keep a watchful eye during meal time.

Blue was a little guy with a big head. He thought he could beat us in a game of tug-of-war. Ha! Did we show him a thing or two! We dragged him all the way across the yard. But...that was not to last for long.

In no time, Blue totally outgrew us. He was part Lab and part Shepherd, so it was a given that he'd get big. Soon, he was dragging *us* across the lawn. We didn't care, it was kind of fun.

Looking back, it's kind of funny how I judged Blazer to be a bully. He is anything *but* a bully. At first, Blazer and I both thought Blue was mean. How could he not be? He looked so different than Blazer and me. Then, we gave him a chance and got to know him. Turns out, he wasn't mean at all. When company would come to the house to see our human, Blue was alright with the dogs they brought along. I mean, he wasn't the best host but...he wasn't nasty to them.

On the other paw, Blue wasn't so hip on people, except for our beloved neighbor, Mary. Every pup, both large and small, loves Mary. When Blue saw Mary he just plopped down and waited for a belly rub. When anyone else came, he would stand guard like he was ready to pounce.

He would get right in between them and me...and Blazer too. I thought he was really rude for doing that until I realized he was just trying to protect us. It's crazy how we misread others when they look different than us or act differently than we do.

There was another odd thing too. Every time our human went to give us a treat (which was pretty often), Blue would close his eyes and brace himself as if he was about to get hit. He did that when our human petted him too.

I thought he was weird. But then, I realized that I had no clue what Blue might have gone through before he joined us. Maybe some mean people had hit Blue. Every single day he makes great progress and becomes more sure that here, he was surrounded by only bunches and bunches of love. Our human had a rule....NO HITTING....EVER! We all liked that rule.

Blue did have a couple issues, though. He had to be the first to eat, the first to go out the door for our walk and the first to do anything we were doing. Initially, that was a problem, especially with Blazer. Then we decided "who cares?" We just let him be first and that is that. Little brothers are just like that sometimes.

Somewhere along the way, the doggie beds fell by the wayside. They got tucked under the bed as we got tucked in the bed. That's right! I got my old spot back.

Every night, I slept with my head on the pillow right next to my human. Once again, I was the princess. Only this time, there were two princes too. How cool is that?

One evening when our human was petting us on the bed, he noticed a little lump on Blue's face. I could tell by my human's eyes that he was worried. A few days later, he took Blue to the veterinarian, whatever that is.

That evening when we heard the car drive up, Blazer and I went to greet our human and Blue. We had missed them both something fierce. But, to our dismay, only our human was there. There was no sign of Blue anywhere. Our human explained to us that Blue had cancer. I wasn't sure what cancer was but I knew it was nothing good.

It seemed like a lifetime before Blue came back home. When he did, we didn't know what to think or do. All he did was lay on the bed all day. Blazer and I were very sad and confused. We were standing beside Blue, with tears rolling down our furry faces. Something amazing happened. Blue looked up at us and jumped down off the bed. He was ready to play. He was as good as new. I'm not positive what a veterinarian is but I like them, I can tell you that much. They made Blue all better.

A few days later, our human came home with yet another dog. She was tiny and pink with curly hair. She looked even more like a princess than I did.

I was crushed. You see, I get my feelings hurt very easily. I thought my human had decided that I was not pretty enough to be the princess of the castle anymore.

I spent the entire evening moping around. I was as sad as sad could be. Why had he replaced me with a prettier princess?

The boys weren't excited about it either. Blazer was sure it meant he was going back to the shelter. Blue realized he might not always get to be first anymore. We simply weren't having it.

Just as we decided that we were being unfair and that if the poor little pup needed a family, we would have to find it in our hearts to give her one, our human's friend came knocking on the door.

"Thank you so much for picking Sweet Pea up," the human said. "And don't you look so pretty?" he said to Sweet Pea. "They always treat you so well."

The human left and took the curly princess dog with him. The three of us breathed a sigh of relief.

In bed that night, our human had a long talk with us. He had sensed we were worried about Sweet Pea joining the family. "I thought it would do you all good to think that for a bit," he said to us. "You guys are the best pups in the world. I am proud of you all for being willing to take her in. You guys don't have to worry though. I think our house and our hearts are full enough. From now on it will just be me, Lily...and the boys."

I looked at my brothers and they looked at me. I whispered so that our human wouldn't hear, "We're the luckiest pups ever, and I'm not even kidding."

Photos of

Lily

The real Mary

Photos of

Blazer

Photos of

Blue

Photos of

"The Pups"

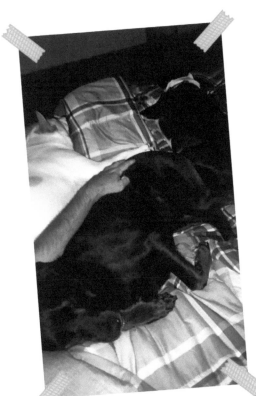

OnPoint Animal Hospital-
Thank You

This book would not be complete unless I say a heartfelt 'Thank You' to the wonderful folks at OnPoint Animal Hospital. They are the caring professionals who maintain the health of the dogs described in this book. They take a sincere interest in each and every animal that they treat, and always patiently answer questions from pet owners. I am truly thankful for the time, effort, and energy they so graciously provide for my sweet babies. I speak for Lily, Blazer, and Blue when I say we feel blessed to be a part of the OnPoint family. Thanks for everything.

(By the way, Blue loves you guys even though he's tried to bite a few of you. He's really sorry.)

ONPOINT
ANIMAL HOSPITAL INC.

CPSIA information can be obtained
at www.ICGtesting.com
Printed in the USA
BVHW02n1046061018
529439BV00004B/34/P